Love,
Alice

a novella

Love, Alice

AMANDA STHERS

Love, Alice

Amanda Sthers

Hardcover ISBN: 978-1-954332-27-0
Paperback ISBN: 978-1-954332-28-7
Library of Congress Control Number on file.

Cover photo by Montypeter | Shutterstock
Black & white illustrations by Wyatt Cleary

Wyatt-MacKenzie Publishing
DEADWOOD, OREGON

for my mom

Dear Sir,

I'm writing this letter because we were never able to tell each other things with words. I didn't speak your language and, now that I've learned the basics, you've left the city. I started taking Japanese lessons after our seventh encounter. It was winter, and the leaves were turning the color I imagine your country being. I wish you could describe Japan so I could understand you along with it.

During my first lesson, my teacher was polite enough not to ask what had inspired me to learn a new language at my age. He simply asked me if there was a particular deadline, and I told him it was that of fate.

"Unmei," he said, and that was the first word your culture offered me.

1

Fate is also what put me on your path, though I'd thought it was foreign to my life. My name is Alice Cendres, but you know me as Alice Renoir. I never explained the mix-up because it didn't seem necessary at first and, as time went by, it would have been strange to unbaptize myself. Later on, I thought I'd been stupid; that it would be impossible for you to find me again if ever you, too, wanted to learn my words the way I'm learning yours, and come tell me what I am about to try to write to you.

I beg you to pay attention to these few pages. They may seem superficial to you in some places, serious or immodest in others, but you'll eventually understand that my life depends on them.

I walked into the tea room last year on October 16th. I keep everything in a notebook, like a kind of almanac that fits in my pocket and sets a rhythm to my life and the few events that punctuate it. I'd have remembered that day without ever writing about it. But I did. Beneath the date I wrote the name of the place, Ukiyo and slipped the tea room's business card inside to be sure to find it again. I now know that the word Ukiyo doesn't exist in my language; that it means to enjoy the moment, outside of the normal course of life, like a bubble of joy. It tells us to savor the moment, detached from our future concerns and the weight of our past. It was four in the afternoon when I walked through the door. Children from the neighboring school were playing in the rain and jumping in puddles while others ran with their school bags on their backs. On mine, I was carrying a life that pained my entire being, but I didn't know it. I smiled, and a young woman who I now know is named Kyoko gestured for me to sit with a slight movement of her lips.

I took off my wet coat and hat. Without my asking, she set a small tray down in front of me with a black teapot and a delicate sky-blue cup that she filled halfway. She explained that the tea came from Miyazaki, the city where I will send you this letter in the morning. I didn't drink it right away—I contented myself with observing the liquid that warmed me; a Futsumushi Sencha with intensely green leaves that produce a beverage with the colors of the sun you see through the tall grass when you're a teenager lying in the meadows. I thought, *There should be a name for this color*, without knowing that a word existed in your world to describe the rays of sunlight scattering through the leaves on trees: *komorebi*. The hue that spreads through the wind and through which you see the most beautiful things.

However, the flavor of this tea isn't as limpid and transparent as its color—it has a density that is somewhat like a liqueur. It tastes a bit like honey softened with bitter cocoa. Forgive my attention to detail, but it's important that you understand that that day changed my life. Not like a sudden impact but more like a wave coming back toward the beach and preparing to turn back again to take on the entire ocean.

I come from a world where we didn't taste exotic things. I only travelled in books, and that's how I became a literature teacher. Perhaps I should have chosen to be a stewardess, to feel real arms around my waist, to kiss faces of other colors. Instead, I never once left the North during my first forty-eight years. I imagined love, people and smells. I found adventure in the comfort of my living room, under a blanket, glued to the pages that I turned incessantly. I've been living in Paris for the last three years, and I'm still scared of not belonging. I moved here at my daughter's request; she married a rich man and "set me up" in a cozy apartment—probably to avoid having to take the train to visit me and the burden of having a mother who doesn't meet the requirements of her new social standing. She thought I was happy to move, whereas I only wanted to make her so. I took a very early retirement and she convinced me that I'd finally "be able to write my novel"—but neither of us truly believed that. It was always a fantasy. She thought that her approach consoled me after her premature arrival and the sacrifices it had meant—that she was giving me back some of the youth she thought she'd stolen from me. But she is the best, most beautiful thing I have ever done. I'm sad that she isn't more afire, that she isn't one of those girls who runs in the rain, laughs, cries and breaks hearts. Those girls who dance barefoot. I never wanted her to give me back my freedom, just to enjoy her own.

When I finished my tea, Kyoko led me up a few stairs and into an adjoining room, saying "Renoir," which she pronounced with an accent that made it impossible for me to understand at first. I thought she was asking me to follow her in Japanese, and I didn't dare refuse. She insisted. She took me into a darker room that was bare—there were only two branches of cherry blossoms in a rectangular vase, a wooden floor, and in the middle, a large, soft surface like the ones in martial arts rooms. On the side, there was a small, lacquered bench on which you could put down your belongings. From her gesture, I understood that I needed to remove my shoes, and I took the navy-blue pajamas she handed me. I was about to protest, but she closed the door with a smile. I thought she was going to give me a massage, that it was included in the tea menu. I didn't dare refuse.

I no longer recall what I was wearing. Probably my black, slightly too-short pants and a grey turtleneck. Nothing worth remembering.

I'd never had a massage. We didn't have a lot of money, and I always put other things first. The body had no place in our lives. We lived in ours to get around, to eat, to have shameful fun or to take a beating; but the idea that it could exist in and of itself wasn't part of my education. I knew I was beautiful after seeing photos of myself years later. I'd never wondered, and no one talked about it. In my world, we did what had to be done. I performed the mechanical movements of existence. I slipped the pajamas on over my bare skin. The rain clattered musically on the slate roof; the gutter beat a cheerful measure. The massage room was in a kind of small, separate house attached to the shop, with a tiny rectangular window high on the wall. I felt as though I was at the end of the world, on an island attached to the rest of Paris. The falling rain soothed me. I was exhausted, but I never talked about it. I was hopeful, I walked fast; my life was borrowing me to do its time more than I was living it. It took my coming there for all of it to hit me, for me to abandon my strength and courage. The minutes I spent waiting for you without knowing it destroyed me.

I didn't know if I should lie down right on the soft surface, so I sat cross-legged in a torpor that made me sway.

When you came in, I was practically anesthetized.

You got down on your knees.

I wasn't expecting to be massaged by a man. Under normal circumstances, I would have objected, but you emanated a gentleness mixed with authority and I was in a fragile state, the object of a story I wasn't writing. The pajama protected me, so, guided by your gestures, I lay down on my back.

You took a moment to join your hands in front of you in the prayer position and then inclined your chest slightly toward the ground. That reassured me, though I didn't really know why—it was as if you were leaving behind your human behaviors to focus solely on my body. And I gave it to you under that thin fabric, whereas no man had touched it for so many years.

You gently took my hand to check my pulse. Your face showed no emotion.

"Cold?"

Yes, I was cold. I nodded my head.

"Tired?"

I hadn't been that tired since I stopped working; but I couldn't answer. I looked at your fingers, so carefully manicured, whereas I'd neglected my own with their chipped polish. I was ashamed for letting myself go. Everything in me expressed exhaustion, so, without waiting for a response, you put your fingers on my eyelids to close my eyes. Then, you took my entire head in your hands. Very delicately, you touched my scalp and gently manipulated its surface, as if to move the ideas around in my head or bring my emotions and hidden dreams to the surface.

Then, you placed your fingers on my neck, and I didn't jump the way I do at every physical contact. You unfolded your fingers. The palms of your hands pressed flat against my skin were warm and open, telling me I had nothing to fear. They molded to the curve of my neck as if they'd been expected and belonged there. Then, you slid them down along my shoulders, over the fragile fabric of the outfit I'd put on, which now took on its full meaning: it wasn't a barrier between us—it was a link. You immobilized your entire body and trained me to match my breathing to yours. We couldn't breathe at different rhythms—your breath asked me to breathe with you, to be with you. And in that duet of exhalations, I was suddenly no longer alone and tears flowed from my eyes. It wasn't sadness, or even emotion; I was simply releasing life. I was bouncing back. I think I fell into a sleeplike state while you worked on my body.

It went on for both a very long time and no time at all. Enough for me to go so far away that I came back to myself—a rebirth, no doubt: steeped in stories beyond my comprehension, yet new.

You left like a ghost without my having time to return your smile. When you left me alone in that room, I felt satisfied and ashamed all at once, as unfaithful women must. I got dressed and paid Kyoko. Tacked onto the mauve wallpaper behind her, I saw her wedding photo taken on the Alexandre III bridge and was thrilled that it wasn't you in her husband's tuxedo. That tinge of jealousy surprised me. I left without running into you, gripped by the cold that contrasted with the warmth in which your hands had enveloped me. I couldn't eat dinner or even think and went to bed almost fully dressed. Alone. Like I do every night. But with the imprint of the memory of your gentle hands.

The next day, I woke up a mess, my hair wavy from perspiration.

I think I had erotic dreams. My cheeks were flushed. My mouth mobile, swollen, and my lips chapped from being bitten. I got up with a need to feel the water from the shower running down my skin for a long time. I'm ashamed to say it, but these last few years, I waited until I smelled to wash. Thanks to you, my body has somehow come back to life. It's warmer, my blood circulates more quickly, and I feel a tingling in my fingertips like a resurrection. At the Paul-Eluard de Roubaix Middle School, where I taught for twenty years, my students said that I made them cold. It was my daughter who'd told me that after an argument. Marine hid the fact that I was her mother, and the kids made fun of me in front of her. We didn't have the same last name. That's all her father left her, that and the darkness of his eyes.

Marine never invited anyone to the house. I wasn't able to throw her a birthday party after 5th grade. She had to hide the fact that she was the Cendres girl. Rid herself of the extinguished fire that marked our family.

"What do they say about me? You can tell me! I'm sure it'll make me laugh. It's fairly normal to laugh at your teachers."

"They say you make them cold."

I never understood whether they thought I wasn't warm, if they saw my discomfort, or if I frightened them. That made me even sadder. In their eyes, I was a November woman, without the lights of Christmas, the joyful resolutions of January, or the last clear skies of October. I made them cold. In the school hallways, I knew they giggled after I passed by. Surely that was normal—students always made fun of their teachers, didn't they? And yet, I wish I could have been an inspiration, throwing them lifelines that would save them from the torment of adolescence, offer them poems as friends, highlight every line of the works that would help them get through life. But then I thought, I'd failed at my own—what advice could I possibly give them? So, I lowered my head and took the bullying.

I didn't think about seeing you again right away. That unexpected episode in my uneventful life could feed my imagination without any need to prolong the reality. I'd surely have hidden it among my embarrassing memories. I'd gone to school with nuns, and anything relating to the body was secondary or embarrassing. And then life had always disappointed me. Second encounters are rarely to my advantage.

And yet, I returned.

The tea room is in my daughter's neighborhood. She lives on one of those chic Paris streets just off of the Champs-Elysées. It's a ten-minute walk from the La Tour-Maubourg metro station on line 8, which I take to go home.

The Saturday after our first encounter—forgive me for writing that, but to me, it was an encounter more than a massage, and I hope I'm not being outrageous by expressing it as such—that Saturday, Marine had invited me to have lunch at her place, and her husband had invited his parents. I'm always very embarrassed to be included in these family reunions—I get the feeling that I don't belong and that people ask me questions as a courtesy. That's why I never say anything interesting in response. I have things to say. If someone showed me any interest, I'd like to surprise them. I know life thanks to literature and entire lines from novels by heart. I've spoken in front of classes that I managed to get interested in *Cyrano de Bergerac* or *La Princesse de Clèves*. Someday, I'd like to tell you about my love for the characters of all the great books that have been my life's companions. But no one talks to me about literature. People ask me if I like it here in Paris. I find this formulation strange and interesting. I don't like it anywhere. I started to like myself in the mirror of the tiny bathroom next to the massage room where I put the medallion of the Virgin back around my neck. I like my face since meeting you.

My daughter's in-laws are older than me, but they have skin that looks like it's made of shiny wax. I think they get Botox injections. They never dare fully smile. He has a lean body. He doesn't like to eat. He doesn't drink. He reads the news carefully and imposes his views on everything. Benoît Lavilaine inherited a steel factory in the Parisian suburbs where it seems his body was made. Incidentally, his eyes are the same shade of dark blue that metal takes on when tempered. He judged me very quickly, thinks that I'm a "hick," and that he's wasting his time with me, but his sense of propriety forces him to respect its use; so, he smiles and is polite and courteous. His wife, Catherine, is a pretty woman who struggles to avoid becoming chubby. Her ankles are thick, as are the pores of her skin. She comes from the provincial middle class, and marrying Benoît Lavilaine was the promotion of her lifetime Catherine refuses to be called Cathy, feels completely Parisian, and wears a suit every day of the week. I know very well that despite Marine's great beauty and excellent education, Catherine had hoped for "better" for her son, no doubt a young woman from a good family, like the fiancé that preceded her. Marine can still pass, but I'm like some kind of idiot. Also, I'm very young, and I can tell that this bothers her— we have nothing in common. I didn't get involved in the wedding plans; I already had a hard-enough time purchasing my daughter a dress, and none of my suggestions found favor in their eyes. At family reunions, I surprise myself by thinking that if you were there, we'd have fun; with one glance, we'd understand each other and play games with our eyes. Without you, I feel like an intruder. I sit on the edges of chairs, never belonging. All of Paris makes me feel this way, but at my daughter's place, it's worse. I only lived a two-hour drive away, but it's as if I've entered a universe I feel I've broke into. Before you, I was dull, like the plaster walls of the living room from my childhood; but suddenly, my few wrinkles have become wildly charming, and I am discovering myself. You gave me back an inner life inhabited by human beings, not heroes in novels.

The lunch was joyful—my daughter's husband announced that she was pregnant. She simply nodded while smiling and caressing her belly. It had been three months already, and I knew nothing about it. I wish she'd told me before the others, that we'd seen each other in private. It seemed strange to me that she had built this fortress with her husband and that I now belonged in the clan of "others." We were no longer one. My sweet little girl, my Marine in pigtails, my little baby girl had left me. I don't think that's what made me angry as I left her place—it was something else: at my age, I was going to become a grandmother and was being asked to find that normal. The rhythm of my life had led me to the absence of flesh, light and hope. I'd behaved like an old woman for so many years that I was seen as one. Suddenly, something in me refused to admit it; in a world where some women my age still bear children, it seemed that the joy of soon becoming a grandmother didn't seem to apply to me. And it was undoubtedly my subconscious this time that, disguised as a coincidence, made me walk past your tea room after that lunch and led me to you once again. In a suspended moment.

Ukiyo.

I was in need of a break that didn't fall within my lifetime.

"Oh, Madame Lenoil!" exclaimed Kyoko. I understood that I'd unwillingly stolen someone else's surname, a woman who must have missed her first appointment and left me her spot. But isn't that what life is always made of? Of masks that you borrow and that end up becoming our face, more real than the real one? I did say to her: "Alice," to at least be partly myself. "My first name is Alice."

And I became Alice Renoir.

Kyoko served me a genmaicha tea. It took me some time to get used to the taste of puffed rice. She informed me that I would have to wait a little while for you to be available for a shiatsu and served me a dorayaki. I thought it was two crêpes stacked on top of each other, but the azuki filling surprised me. It was a taste of someone else's childhood in a faraway country—you were offering me your madeleine, your colors, your memories. The combination of the tea and the red bean cake gives off the aroma of dates, and I suddenly remembered the ones sold by the grocer that lived on the corner, which he'd offered us with walnuts for the New Year. They came from his village in Tunisia and melted in my mouth just like this brown paste. I also remembered the taste of chestnut cream, which I didn't like putting in yogurt but that I swallowed by the spoonful so the sugar would fill me and tickle the back of my throat. All the sweet childhood memories bombarded me. I was going to be a grandmother, and I became aware of the atrocious joy that was too much, that filled my mouth like syrup, and I was afraid and sickened. I was angry. Sickened to the point of vomiting. I wondered where my life had gone, the one I hadn't dared to start. I still had the ticket for a ride on a carousel that went around and round, without my ever being able to get on; and now night was beginning to fall, the carousel was slowing down, and the theme park was closing in on me.

When I came to you, I was full of a dull and shameful rage.

Once again, you leaned your chest toward me with your hands joined together. I've since learned from reading books on shiatsu that this salutation is called "gasshô"; that it's a means of creating a bond with the patient to form a chorus, like children that sing together in a church to reach God.

There is something divine in your hands, in the gestures that you repeated as if they were ancestral—of which you were merely the legatee—and you were transferring the weight lifted from past bodies and their light to my body so as to heal me.

What is your religion?

Are you a Buddhist? I asked Kyoko. She told me you followed Shintoism of which I knew nothing before doing some research and that I admit I don't entirely understand. It seems to me that it's an animistic religion, like the ones you find in Africa; a cult from the beginning of time, that gives life rhythm more that it does any order, a sort of gentle belief that makes life hard because there is no promise of the afterlife, no divine plan—just an idea of the soul and its recurrences over time. Praise of what has been and continues to be invisible in an abstract world that survives thanks to what we leave behind and what lies ahead to lose us forever. It's basically a religion of melancholy writers. And it suits you well; I thought that you must also pray like Kyoko in a deeply moving silence.

You felt my energy. You said, "No good." And you shook your hands downward after touching me as if to rid yourself of all the bad vibes I was carrying. So, your hands started their dance on my skull again. It hurt. It felt good. A sort of masochistic delight. My entire body relaxed, my thighs spread, and I flattened myself against the ground, which drew me in. I fell asleep like a child, my muscles shamelessly relaxed. And I dare to say it now: I wanted you when I drifted off to sleep. Wanted you to enter me and never come back out. Wanted you to take me like a fortress; I felt besieged and ready lay down my weapons, ready to submit to your power.

When I woke up, you were no longer there. I think I snored. I got dressed quickly. After I left, I went to the bistro around the corner to eat a peppered steak despite the sugar from the cake that was still stuck to my palate. My appetite had returned, too. Life, in other words. I can't say that I was wounded, but certainly numb, impervious to the chaos of love, a stranger to desire, distant. As if this thing, neither soiled nor sublimated, was simply no longer capable of affecting me. Another person within me had decided that I should avoid it. I think I know when this shift happened; just after a man with whom I'd fallen head over heels in love with and who loved me in return decided that, despite the joy he felt spending time with me and the wit he found in me, he didn't want to kiss me full on the mouth. Sure, he made love to me occasionally, but with his eyes turned upward, probably concentrating on the image of another woman. So, I got fed up. I left. I could almost understand it—my body was disgusting: heavy, sagging breasts, wide hips, slim ankles and a thin face, as if it had been planted on a trunk that was carrying too much weight, too many memories. But you know its contours better than me. Beneath your hands, I almost started to like it and lost weight over time although I was eating a lot more. Probably because I felt life returning to the box that protects my heart, which you made me want to hear beating again. I felt not that I was living my life so much as having been lived by it. For the time I have left, I'd like to be the hand guiding the old, creaking, wooden puppet that I am, that continues to grow and is starting to hope that it can escape. You should know all about me, so that I can listen to you in turn, and so that we can love each other in silence as we have since the beginning. With you, everything has come back to me. By silencing my body, my feelings, closed pores, food without enjoyment, nights without love, I silenced a part of my memories, no doubt to forget. Now, I want to relieve myself of them through these lines and run all the way to Myazaki. I remember that, as a child, I'd watch birds flying and I wondered if the wind carried them like dead leaves to seduce the sky or if they were the ones playing with it.

That day, I waited for you at the bus stop so I could follow you home. I'm ashamed to admit this to you. I wanted to know where you lived, if you went home to a wife or children. If you dined alone. If you smiled while talking on your cell phone. If you hummed to yourself. If there was room for me in your life. I didn't admit any of this to myself; I told myself you were the character in the famous novel I dreamed of writing; that what attracted me was a mystery that would work on readers because it had worked on me. It was snowing. The flakes weren't sticking and turned into a kind of black mud. I was cold. I should have gone home a thousand times, but after a certain point, the effort I'd put in was too great to give up—I told myself that I hadn't waited all that time for nothing. So, despite my frozen limbs, I stayed until night fell, and, a few hours after that, you helped Kyoko with the iron curtain. I felt ridiculous watching you from afar. What would I have said to you had our eyes met? A car honked and Kyoko turned around—it was her husband in an old, green Peugeot. He wasn't wearing the tuxedo from the photo, but I recognized his wide smile. You both got in and he started the engine. I stayed there alone like an idiot with wet feet in that frigid bus stop shelter. I took a taxi. I caught a flu that kept me bedridden for almost a month.

In your eyes, which I dared to look into at our third encounter, there is a gentle, immutable melancholy. This time, I made an appointment. I'd said "Alice" over the phone and Kyoko had answered, "Oh Madame Lenoil, of kos." There was an opening just before noon. The year was coming to an end and it was still snowing; but this time, a blanket of white gave a fairytale charm to all of Paris, which was sprinkled with lights for the coming holidays. It took me a month to admit that I wanted to see you again, that it wasn't just a massage. We can sense who the people that touch us physically are, their emotions. There are traces of what we are in our skin—it emanates from our flesh like a scent of our cruelty or, on the contrary, our kindness, as is the case with you. At the end of our massages, the scent of your skin on mine was like a bandage, and it combined with my scent to create another: us. I know you as if we've spoken for a long time. I dare to think so. I also know that you haven't been happy; only a broken being can heal another. We only understand pain if we've spent time with it.

I am that woman in the long coat who waited with you for Kyoko to arrive that December morning. The metro wasn't down because of bad weather; only Kyoko had the key, and we met at the entrance of the tea room. You were wearing a kind of soft suit that closed on both the inside and outside as I noticed when, after a moment, you nodded to suggest the café next door. I followed you. You ordered. You were wearing several thin sweaters, one over the other, as if you were in pajamas, and that did something to me.

"Coffee, please."

You gestured for two, your fingers spread widely. We'd barely drunk them, embarrassed at not being able to say anything and saying too much with our awkward silences, when Kyoko arrived, running with her childlike smile that turned downward—like a smiley face that's happy and sad at the same time. We followed her. You left me alone for a long while before coming into the room so I'd forget that you lived a life outside of this place, so that I'd only ever visualize you as a masseur, so that I would forget your features when I left. It didn't work. For the first time, I saw the details of your face. A wide mouth. A long, slender nose with symmetrical nostrils. There is a tiny scar under your right eye—it's shaped like a tear. You seldom open your mouth; you hide your smile. At first, I'd thought that your teeth, which overlap a little, embarrassed you. But since Kyoko always graciously covers her laugh with her hand, I wondered if it wasn't some form of Japanese politeness.

Yes, I'm Alice, Alice from the café, whose fingers you grazed when we both reached for a sugar cube at the same time.

In the room, you touched my body and it was normal and allowed; but in that café, it became taboo. So, when our hands brushed against each other in the sugar bowl, I was confused.

I am that woman—do you know who I am?

I'm afraid that I imagined everything, that to you I am just one person among many.

I'm writing all of these emotions, this intimacy, to you.

Am I ridiculous? Should I mail this letter?

I don't know if you should read it, but I have no choice but to write it.

Otherwise, I'll choke on all of these words.

I hope you'll read this in one sitting, but I need time to write it—it's been devouring me for nights.

When I get too emotional, I put down my pen.

After that third encounter, I looked up "Japanese lessons" on the Internet. I ended up on a tiny street in the 11th arrondissement where a door opens onto a courtyard hallway in which there are several artists' workshops. My teacher shares one with a bird seller. Her name is Simone and she trains birds for their owners and also sells some rare pearls. She is specialized in "inseparables," the species of bird that looks for his soul mate and never leaves again once he's found her.

So, it was in the midst of more or less charming chirps that I learned to speak the language that connects us. My Japanese teacher is called Roger. It's a strange name for a twenty-year-old man born in Osaka, but his father was taken with Brigitte Bardot and a big Francophile, so he inherited his first name from Roger Vadim, the actress' first husband, along with a perfect mastery of the language after he himself fell in love with that ass while watching *Le Mépris* one prepubescent evening. Roger Tanaka has a face that is round like the cakes that Kyoko serves me in your tea room. His skin is flawless and he wears large, square glasses that decorate his small, laughing eyes. I get the feeling he knows everything and has figured out exactly what I'm doing here. I'm working hard so I can talk to you, but also to show him that I'm not some flighty, inconsequential bird. He told me that of all the adults, I was his most applied student. There's a child who learns much faster than me, a little brat with pigtails who started lessons at the same time but already talks to him, making jokes, while I struggle to pronounce the words. Pauline. I loathe her. We run into each other on Wednesdays, and she is very mean. I brought her snacks to soften her up; she eats them, and then, once they're all gone, looks me square in the eyes and says: "It wasn't good."

Roger Tanaka is stickler for cleanliness. When we arrive, we have to take off our shoes, slip on these wooden slippers and carefully wash our hands. Roger hasn't told me much about Osaka; only that all over the country, the Japanese move to the left on escalators, as they do when driving, to let those who wish to go faster overtake them. It's very organized. Osaka is the only exception; they stand on the right side of escalators "like in France!" he told me proudly, as if that explained his entire journey and arrival in Paris.

"Most Samurais were right-handed and wore their swords on the left. The same was true for the knights of England, which is why it has remained so."

And no one carried a sword in France or in Osaka?

"Yes," he replied, basking in the effect, "but France moved 'the weapon to the right' after Napoleon changed the law to piss off the English."

And he laughed, half-embarrassed, half-proud over using a vulgar word and its little effects. You could tell that he loved to tell this little anecdote.

"Whereas, in Osaka, we were a city of merchants and not warriors, and if the swords were carried on the left, the purses were carried on the right."

Roger Tanaka likes to say that History has a sense of humor. I don't share his opinion, but I don't want to get angry with him. Throughout this year of lessons, Roger Tanaka has taught me a lot more than the country's language. He invited me to have lunch in a traditional restaurant to celebrate my fiftieth lesson. I don't know much about him, but I think he's homosexual. I'm not sure that he knows it or that he's dared to admit it to himself. Roger talks about chivalrous love, the kind he's read about in novels. When I ask him if he's ever loved or been loved, he hides his embarrassed laugh as if he were a teenager and replies, "Oh no, love isn't for Roger," without looking sad. We tasted the great imperial and traditional Kaiseki cuisine and drank a lot of sake. We went outside drunk and sang French songs in the street. Roger listened to Claude François with his father.

I don't know if you know him, but he is one of our idols who died young. Few people know that *My Way* was originally French and was called *Comme d'habitude*. If we see each other again someday, I'll play it for you. My favorite is called *Magnolias Forever* and when he sings my eyes well up. I've always had a very intimate relationship with music. I don't think of it as just a distraction—it affects me deeply. Roger and I had a good laugh and cried while singing about the lives we weren't living in the streets of Paris at night.

Roger showed me another form of music and introduced me to haiku. Of course, I had already read some, but I don't think I understood this poetic form before being able to read them in Japanese.

Roger told me that all stories and all moments could exist in these three suspended phrases.

"Give it a try, Madame Alice."

I twirl the pen between my fingers.

"Who inspired you to learn Japanese?"

The sound of the rain
My footsteps also laughing
Awaken my fate.

My young teacher nods his head and we move on to something else. His modesty envelops me with relief. At Roger's suggestion, I bought some works of Japanese literature. I knew almost nothing aside from Murakami. The day after our celebratory evening, I opened *The Tale of Genji*, Murasaki Shikibu's masterpiece, the way you slowly open the wrapping paper on a gift. A few days after that delicious reading experience, I found out that Murasaki Shikibu was a woman. And yet, this sensual tornado was written around 1005 and the main character is a prince with a thousand mistresses. How your culture surprises me with its mixture of archaism and open-mindedness! The romantic and political intrigues in the court of Heian are the result of women maneuvering behind screens like shadows of desire. I couldn't stop myself after that and read Kenzaburō Ōe... and *House of the Sleeping Beauties* by Kawabata. I thought that those young geishas sleeping in a brothel so that old men could look at them the way one does at lost youth were speaking to me about my life, the time I let go by—knowingly, yes, but unable to offer myself better for fear of suffering. I read the repeated damnations in each of the works by Mishima, *In Praise of Shadows* by Tanazaki and the art of not showing everything, and Natsume Sōseki as well. For each work, I had the Japanese version and the adaptation. I tried to read everything in Japanese, but it was still too complicated— particularly because of the rhythm, emotions, and the ideas; everything I learned in French literature differed on all counts. Where the writings that built your literature shift between aestheticism and perversity, ours are made up of impossible loves and damnation. This made me understand that I was foreign to your culture, that everything separated us except our humanity and your hands that saved my skin.

In Japanese, all is a kind of melancholy that makes death sweet. Transience is what seems to produce the most powerful emotions. Delight is found in the specification of each and every thing. Knowing what I am not is teaching me so much about myself. I keep reading about your country in the metro and dreaming of us between the pages.

On Thursday, January 19th, I missed my station because I was lost in the middle of *The Pillow Book* by Sei Shōnagon and the delicate splendors of the Heian civilization—far from Lamarck-Caulaincourt, where people rushed around in clusters, their shoes covered in melted snow that transformed the sidewalks into slush. I wrote that down in my notebook. I had to walk through the corridors once again to change direction. I decided to look up so I wouldn't end up at the terminus. I observed a weathered-looking man sitting across from me and found him handsome. Then I thought to myself that if those same wrinkles were on a woman, her face would be judged "interesting" without assigning her any seduction power. Women's skin ages objectively better; but novels, films, and artistic representations have always represented the women that inspire desire as young, innocent, almost stupid. The men who built these myths have offered themselves the best role for years and deny my desire, my sexuality, and my femininity, which may last. Up until now, I accepted the weight of what I was taught and the fact that I was going to die and should give up my seat for newcomers, with their firm breasts and fresh ova. Forgive me for speaking this way, but it struck me rather violently. I was angry and blamed myself for not allowing my own right to desire. It's very hard for me to write this, and I am ashamed of it, but one day I caught your gaze lingering on the curves of my body. I didn't dare lower mine to your pants, but we are animals, and we know these things. Please don't be ashamed or feel attacked by what I am telling you or about all of the times that I saw you. Instead, take this as my ability to look at you as a whole, just as you are.

For you to understand me, you need to know me better. I'm going to tell you pieces of my life so that you know who I am, and you can welcome me without falsehood or shut the door forever. I won't spare you any of the truth or my quirks—that way, we'll know if we can hope for mine to coexist with yours. From my childhood, I remember the boredom, but not really its lasting over time. God knows there were long, empty days. I didn't grow up in a family that took vacations; we had endless summers. It was hot, even in the North. Sometimes, my grandfather would take us to the beach for the day, along with my cousin and his dog. The trips back and forth felt like an eternity to me; everything was long and similar, like the endless beaches in Wissant between cape Blanc-Nez and cape Gris-Nez. In good weather, you could see the English coastline, and it made the landscape even bigger. There were drawings in the hot sand that frightened me. The water was freezing, the contrast startling. I still preferred boredom over all of these sensations; in my bedroom, I could at least live inside a book borrowed from the library. That landscape that I knew so well, I loved it as described by Victor Hugo; those words enabled me to understand its beauty much later. Our grandfather gave us a little money and then left to "attend to his business" before coming back to get us at night when he smelled of alcohol and ladies' perfume. He died on that road one day when we weren't in the car to keep him awake. My father loved to say that the cassette player stayed stuck on *Voyage, voyage*, a song that was popular in the eighties. My father said repeatedly, "He wanted to travel, he couldn't go any farther," and seemed to find that funny.

Please excuse the disorder in which I'm telling my story—I don't get the feeling that we're the outcome of a straight line; instead, we're attached to a multitude of strings like puppets that move about. I don't know what my puppet looks like, surely not like a princess; and yet, I believe that my heart is pure. How do I tell you about myself when I've kept so quiet that I didn't acknowledge my own desires? Where do I start?

I'm one of those people who is afraid. When I walk into a room, I'm uncomfortable. I don't envy the people who move through the world as if in a domain scaled to their dimensions; but I would so like to know what that feels like. I'm clumsy, I bump into things, I drop whatever I'm holding in my hands. My hair forms messy curls, so I put it in a chignon. People think I'm stern, but I'm muddled. If I show myself as I am, people will surely see that I'm a lost child.

When I think about it, I tell myself that everything came to a halt for me in my eighth winter; that I've remained stuck on that day, the day my innocence ended, in my cotton nightgown that wasn't warm enough. I know it. But I refuse to think about it. That would mean dying. Yes, dying.

And the snow that falls
The slow silence of gestures
The cloth of childhood.

So, I'm telling you this way, but I won't tell you the story. In Cambrai, sadness lived in my neighborhood. It belonged to its residents like it did to the sparse trees, the dirty bus shelters or the color of the sky that was seldom blue. When you speak of Cambrai, people think of *bêtises de Cambrai*, and it becomes charming. Do you know about bêtises de Cambrai? This candy was the result of a mistake made by Emile, a baker's boy. While he was making mint candies, he added the wrong amounts of sugar and mint and, in a panic, blew air into the mixture. When he saw the result, the confectioner exclaimed: "Look at this nonsense!"

My daughter loved for me to tell her this story when she was a child. It was reassuring to know that mistakes can have a marvelous taste and even become a recipe, the rule, an institution! Like our encounter, it took so many mistakes to fulfill our destiny. I'd like to offer you a box of bêtises if you invite me to visit you.

Cambrai has its charm: on Aristide Briand square, there are lovely houses that look as though they're made of gingerbread. My grandfather explained to me that the square, which was destroyed during the First World War, was rebuilt and, in the process, its uneven sides were corrected. At the time, I'd told myself that something good can come from every tragedy and, with my childish instincts, I knew that someday someone would rebuild me, too. Or at least, I began to hope for that, and it was enough to keep me alive.

You see, from the bêtises de Cambrai to Aristide Briand square, all of the images from my childhood told me that the darkest life could be illuminated or take on the charm of its shadow. Since then, nothing has changed. Even the faces seem intact in my town in the North. In the preface to *Notre Dame de Paris*, Victor Hugo makes the connection between language and architecture. These big cities, stormed, rebuilt, carved up, in constant movement, authorize the transformation of the language and its vitality – an adapted word, because the evolution of a language also leads to its death. For me, a French teacher from the North stuck in an unchanging manner of speaking, Paris makes too much noise. Learning Japanese lets me slow my life down and not feel pushed toward the precipice to which every metro corridor, every street, every commotion of Paris leads. I admire the fact that your island is resisting the illness of globalization, that you're keeping your traditions, your differences. I learned from Roger Tanaka that you have giant fruits in your markets, that students and teachers clean up the schools themselves, that the seats on your toilets are heated, and the ones in trains can be turned around completely so that you're always facing the direction in which you're travelling. Also, the Japanese apparently don't kiss in public or hold hands. And yet, in my dreams, we went to dinner several times and you opened the door for me, let me walk in ahead while caressing my back discreetly... Then, we went dancing; always in the same wood-paneled ballroom with no windows. I don't know what city we're in, or which country.

If you enter the world of my childhood, you will find the house at number 8 on Grande Rue Verte unchanged. We lived in a little house that my father inherited, and divided into two apartments. We lived in the one on the ground floor. The upstairs neighbors came through our door to enter and access the stairs. At dinner time, we lowered our voices when we heard the door open. Depending on the rhythm and the weight of the person walking, we knew who was coming in. At certain times, it was Mrs. Yves who stumbled, and I'd have sworn I could smell her inebriated breath all the way from my bed. So, I hid under the sheets and waited for her husband's shouts to be sure she'd made it upstairs and wasn't going to come into my room. Mrs. Yves was nice, but even her kindness frightened me; her bulging eyes hid an immense reserve of tears that were ready to flow. The sadness of others has always seemed disgusting to me, and I don't know what to do with it. I comfort others by offering the mirror of my own silent suffering. They had two children. Their daughter, Marilyn, whose real name was Josie and who was as fleshy as her mother was thin, had cleavage that spilled out of her dress. She let my father feel her up. On several occasions, I saw him grab a breast, take it out of her top and massage it indelicately, the way a child plays with modeling clay. I don't know which of the two that satisfied, or what their arrangement was, but they repeated their game like a ritual. I never saw them exchange a kiss or a passionate look, just a deep grope of a tit. Their son was older and in the army. And I think I was in love with him. On nights when he was on leave, when I heard him come in, I couldn't go to sleep. I listened for his voice above my bedroom. And I'd go to serve myself glasses of water in the hopes that he would come down at the same time in his fitted uniform. He smoked at the window and gave me a vague greeting whenever our eyes met. That was it, and it was enough for me to think about him for weeks. In my diary, I called him "the soldier," and I drew hearts near the words that were about him.

My parents were drowning in debt. When they died within a year of each other, I didn't inherit the house, and that was a relief. Why did I have the impression that the street behind ours was so joyful? That we lived in a kind of diabolical triangle that couldn't give birth to happy lives? My high school friends and I called it "Bermuda." Every night, I returned to a danger zone, a place where destinies were sucked in and destroyed.

Unmei. That's why I didn't think that another life could exist within mine aside from my own. An unexpected face. A different culture. A different color of brick, clouds and soil. For a thing to exist, you had to be able to touch it. We didn't think about those who were absent; we loved the people who appeared on television. My family didn't understand the heroes in novels or the fact that those fictitious people could make me cry. I was a strange girl to all of them!

Daddy's name was Bernard. He was a logger, and he was illiterate. Back then, they were called "logger-piece-workers" because they were paid on a project basis by sawmills or logging companies. My father took his tools and went on assignments. Those were happy moments. I'd hear my mother sing, we ate a bit later; without anything being said, his absence took on a festive feel. Daddy cut down trees and I read books. I probably needed to ascribe some meaning to his life, which had none. He was the link in a weak chain, the mobile DNA of useless mankind, and I was his daughter. An ant that carried nothing to the next. That is what I understood from reading the myth of Sisyphus. I'd planned to not bother pushing a stone to the top of the mountain; I wanted everything to end with me; to not have a family, to die and let this miserable part of humanity that I was perpetuating die out. But you don't decide to become a feline when you're an ant, and I got pregnant. Like everyone. I wanted a man. I was still a teenager, and he was like most men: a coward. Never lower your guard before the brazen beauty of those who are sure of themselves, who know how to make scrolls of cigarette smoke float past their eyes, who aren't afraid of anything.

There was a jukebox in the bar next to the house. It was the only place where I could listen to songs. How I loved that! The music took over my body, but I held back from dancing. I learned the lyrics by heart, sang them silently in my head on the way back home, and I danced, danced in my bedroom trying not to make any noise. On my tiptoes. It was 1987. INXS' *Need You Tonight*. Michael Jackson's *Bad*. Madonna's *Papa Don't Preach*. And Jean-Jacques Goldman's *Elle a fait un bébé toute seule*...

He walked into the bar during George Michael's *I Want Your Sex*.

The lyrics of those songs warned me of what was to come, but all I wanted when I looked into his eyes was to be his. I thought I'd understood love in an instant, because it was obviously linked to desire. How could it have been otherwise?

I stole money from my mother's purse, put on fishnet stockings and bows in my hair. At first, he didn't pay any attention to me, or so little that it had to be intentional. I ordered alcoholic drinks, forced my gestures and laughter. Everything was coarse. My exaggeration seemed to increase my transparency. One night, I snuck out yet again but couldn't find a girlfriend to go with me. I walked into the bar as he was kissing a girl full on the mouth. Undaunted, I sat down to drink. The sadness swelled, my mind set off for a sad country for what must have been a long time. I didn't see him coming and his hand on my shoulder made me jump.

"Are we sad tonight?"

I didn't answer. He'd never spoken to me before.

"Come on," he said.

And I followed him. He held the tip of my hand, like a light thread, and I ran so he wouldn't let go of it. I had trouble walking in the too-high heels of my grown woman's disguise. We went to his place. He undressed me without kissing me, the way you open a package sent by the post office to find out if it's a present or bad news. It was so long ago, and yet I remember everything. I don't dare tell you what he asked me, but he quickly understood that I had no experience. He explained:

"Like that. That's good. No, not so fast."]

He sometimes laughed at my clumsiness.

"I'm going to make you better. You'll come here and I'll teach you."

And I was flattered.

I hadn't read Beauvoir. That same year, Elisabeth Badinter wrote *L'un est l'autre* in a civilized sphere while I was being taught to submit like livestock on a farm. Like all teenagers of my generation, things didn't need to be organized for us to obey them. We'd all grown up in the idea of these norms. I was far from thinking that what I was experiencing was ugly. Ready to take everything that this man gave me—hip nudges and punches, both low and twisted. Everything. He never asked me if I liked what he was doing to me; but he told me when I made him feel good, and that had to be enough. I'd been raised to believe that a woman had to carry out certain tasks. It was never said out loud, but in that culture of silence, I heard my mother's submissiveness—her "duty to perform." I was sixteen.

What I am writing to you is reminding me of things that I have never talked about. That hurt me. Sometimes, in my imagination, I go away to comforting countries that wrap me up in cotton bandages. I leave reality and, while I'm floating, I have no idea how quickly time is going by or if it is going by at all.

After six months of lessons, Roger Tanaka, who had noticed my distractibility, imposed a minute of meditation before the start of each lesson. He no longer spoke to me in anything other than Japanese. During that minute, I had to make room for another version myself and forget my own language. If I was at a loss for words, he asked me to think in images and then do drawings. The lessons resembled a game of Pictionary, and sometimes I learned a word that just missed being an elephant's trunk instead of a fire hose. If I make mistakes, I can't get angry with myself. I am like a little girl who's learning with a book of scribbled images.

I wonder what your childhood was like in Japan. What music did you listen to? Did you rewind cassette tapes with ballpoint pens? And your hairstyles? Were they like ours? Did girls set themselves free with Madonna, sporting teased manes and smoky eyes that rubbed off on the tarnished destinies that life had once promised? What did your first love look like? Do you have any children? I'm not judging you; I'm simply asking questions to get to know you. I wonder how my life would have gone had I been the master of it.

After a few months of obeying Alexis' desires, I watched my belly grow with amazement. I didn't say anything because it couldn't be real—I thought that something would save me from this accident, that one morning I'd wake up and everything would be back to normal.

On my seventeenth birthday, my parents found out. They'd given me a swimsuit to go to my aunt's in Touquet and insisted that I try it on. I didn't want to, and my father told me:

"Try it on right now! It was expensive. Try it on and show us!"

I went into my bedroom and slipped on the one-piece swimsuit made of blue gingham fabric.

I didn't have a mirror, but my belly had swollen and already I couldn't see my privates. My breasts looked almost like Marilyn's and hurt.

I took a long time.

My father shouted:

"So?"

Finally, I came out of my bedroom.

They looked at me, my father smiled: "You're becoming a woman, you're really filling out."

I looked up at my mother who understood.

"My God, my God, this isn't happening. Jesus, Mary and Joseph, not you! Not my little girl!"

Then, my father's eyes turned to my belly.

My mother prayed.

He got up and slapped me. Hard enough to knock me on the floor. I protected my belly. He kept going. My mother murmured prayers through her tears and he turned to tell her to be quiet, that her righteousness wasn't going to save us from anything. So, I took advantage of the moment to run away and escape his blows. I crawled then ran to the front door, grabbed a coat— my father's—and went out.

I ran into the neighbor in his soldier's uniform, a cigarette in his mouth. "The handsome soldier"; I thought, if my friends could see this ... he mumbled a hello. My lip was bloodied. He pretended not to notice. He caressed my head, but not with desire—the way you pat a dog that you want to reward—and walked on. I thought, "I have to wait for him, he'll protect me, I'm sure of it." I turned back around and sat on the front steps. When the soldier came back drunk a few hours later, I was cold and curled up in a ball beneath that enormous, fragile coat that covered my swimsuit.

He opened the door for me, but instead of letting me go toward my apartment, he grabbed my hand and walked me up the stairs. It was like a dream that I'd had so many times, but with the wrong colors and smells, which didn't fit with the imagined scenario. He pushed me onto his bed. He didn't pay any attention to my belly at first. It was afterward—after taking me without permission, that he told me, "You're a real slut, aren't you," looking at my stretched navel and understanding that I was pregnant. I still had the scent of a child.

Time doesn't go by
It pushes hard against me
And I escape it.

Men have had me at their disposal. I have never known any kind gestures. I know that yours are professional and I'm not confused by them. And yet, I feel like there is something we have that is bigger than us.

I'd be ashamed if I was wrong. Please tell me so directly if that is the case.

In March, while I refused to let myself believe that

you could feel anything whatsoever for me, one gesture made me think otherwise. I'd put on my jacket and was about to leave when you said, "Alice." I turned around and you looked directly into my eyes. I could barely respond. I already knew how to say yes in Japanese and might have tried it, but my heart was childishly aflutter and my cheeks must have turned red.

"I don't know if you're familiar with these pieces of paper that we fold to create shapes. We call them origamis. I made this one for you."

You said it in perfect French. I know that it was a challenge. You must have learned those sentences and practiced them out loud while thinking about me as you went back over each fold the same way that you focus on relaxing my skin beneath this light pajama. That paper object was nothing, but it was proof that I existed somewhere other than this room, that I followed you home, that I lived in a small space in your imagination.

That origami is watching me as I write to you, and giving me courage.

It's a crane. I looked it up. It's a traditional gift with no romantic symbolism. But I unfolded and refolded it to see how much time it took you to make this present before you dropped it off with your usual delicacy so it seemed trivial. I understood that you'd made an effort. And, I admit it, I also wanted to know if the crane hid a clue, a love letter, a trace of perfume or simply the folds made by a man who was thinking of me.

I see I'm getting lost in the memories that connect us. As soon as I start sinking into the darker moments of my life, I grab onto this life preserver that is saving me from what broke me. Psychoanalysts say that we construct ourselves based on our pain, too; that the flaws are our bones; but I only see them as fractures. Can I remember the helpless young girl who found herself pregnant, beaten, and isolated in her books with parents who had trouble deciphering three words, without thinking about the dejection that accompanied my life? I understood what survival was when my father kicked me out. One of his friends took me in when I was on the verge of freezing to death in a doorway. I hadn't eaten in two days. I kept moving for a long time; I'd walked at night to keep from freezing or being spotted by other vagrants who frightened me. That friend slipped a scarf around my neck and took me by the hand. He was a little older than Daddy. He had a benevolent grandfather face. What kindness, I thought at first; but then he made it clear that I couldn't stay for free and that he found me pretty. One morning before going out to buy food, he made me a proposal: we only had to be intimate once a week—the rest of the time, he'd be satisfied just holding my hand in front of the television. He was embarrassed to say this to me, and there was foamy drool in the corners of his mouth. He left for the market with his basket, and without even thinking to take a warm sweater from his closet, I fled. Marie spotted me in the street. I was lost. I'd taken my little backpack and put my coat on over my nightgown. I was crying. Marie was in charge of an association. She took me by the shoulders and I jumped, ready to bite. She held on and offered me a hot chocolate. I told her my story. She had an unattractive face but a sweet voice that you couldn't forget. I lived in a home for young women, and my mother came in secret to bring me money and food. I never stopped going to school and it saved me. After my first year of teacher's school, I met a good man. His name was Antonin. He saw me at the supermarket, counting coins to buy milk—I couldn't breastfeed Marine anymore as she went to daycare and I was working as a waitress after school. He came over and paid for the milk. He didn't offer to because I would have refused, he simply took out the money as if we'd shopped together. Then, he carried my groceries, and we went to pick up my daughter. It was all natural, easy.

Antonin made me feel like I was going home; that imaginary refuge that had saved me on cold days. He had an almost mobile face with no specific features, the kind you have a hard time remembering. In fact, when I close my eyes now, I can't remember him, so I look at a photo that I've kept, and it all comes back to me. The three of us are sitting on the orange sofa in his living room. Marine is smiling, and you can see her three front milk teeth, which make her look like a mouse. We look happy. Antonin opened his arms to me, but he never made love to me. He took care of me and my daughter like cats he'd adopted from an animal shelter. Little by little, desire burgeoned, but Antonin refused my few clumsy attempts. At night, he kissed my forehead. My tears flowed in silence. Two years later, my father died and I was able to go back home. I never saw the soldier again, but I trembled at every step. I'd been defiled or ignored and deformed by pregnancy before I'd even become a woman. I felt dirty and ugly, and I rejected my body. Antonin tried to catch me, but his tenderness resembled a prison, and I wept at the idea of what we could have been. In Cambrai, I often went to Antonin's—he was probably my first love. It was as if another version of me lived there happily, in a world where my life would have been good. I hope to run into myself one day, hold me in my arms and disappear into that other Alice—blend into her happy life full of friends, closed parentheses, kitchen aromas and chipped glasses from too many parties. Does a woman live in that house? Did she take my share of happiness?

If you only knew how alone I am. The more people there are around me, the deeper I sink into the certainty of not belonging to this whole. I need your hands on my skin, to heal beneath your warm palms, to have you finally remove this fabric that separates us so I can be yours completely and experience the taste of the sweet life. I don't want to hold onto our meeting like some beautiful object that you store inside a box. I've done that my entire existence, and this time I want to live, feel your torso, your breath close to mine, the night that devours us and that we spend together. Since meeting you, I close the shutters, turn off the lights, and dance for hours in secret. I hadn't done that since I was a teenager. The rhythm seeping into my movements helps me enter a kind of trance, and I have the feeling that you are inside me.

The sun is setting. I've spent the day poring over this page, but I can't bring myself to leave us. I'm telling you so many things, and I should resist this outpouring; the few friends I have left living in Lille would tell me to hold back, to remain mysterious; but, you see, I haven't been able to accept the modern illness of nonchalance. How do you hide your feelings from someone you love? If we hold back, it means the heart is no longer at the helm, that the mind has taken over—that we're going into battle.

There were many times that I wanted to believe in true love, and it made a fool of me. I'm discovering Kawabata's tiny novels, those stories that fit into the palm of your hand but tell you everything about a life.

I feel close to him. To his solitude. The larger the crowd, the more he feels alone; and yet, he feels no animosity toward others. He brushes past them, moves ahead, sinks into the darkness of his existence. Even his suicidal characters seem to like people. I see myself in this contradiction; I don't wish anyone harm, but I wish someone had been good to me. I never dared to ask. It seems that the more I gave, the more they ran away from me, that love is wanting the other's skin, first through wild lovemaking; then, after the truce and the exhaustion brought on by the state of being in love, comes a second energy. Then, we want each other's skin on a scaffold of rebukes, sadness, and telephones that no longer ring.

I'm going to bed—dawn must already be caressing your eyelids. I wonder how you'll open the envelope in which these pages will hide. Will a postman slip it into the mailbox in front of your house? Will he put it directly in your hands with a broad smile? I'll probably put perfume on it. Will the lily scent survive the journey? Will you read this letter in one go or slowly, like the well-behaved children that open one surprise per day from their advent calendars? Do you have those in Japan? They're little houses that hold gifts or chocolate behind their windows and separate us from Christmas Day—the December countdown. Yours must be so delicate, like everything I'm discovering about your country. When I dream of Japan, I imagine a long autumn day with trees that are red like the ones in the botanical gardens of the Manoir-aux-Loups. I took Marine for walks there when she was a little girl. She was so pretty; people stopped me to tell me so, and everyone smiled at her.

I admit I can't get over no longer being a full-time mother, no longer worrying about her welfare. No longer being responsible for another soul makes my own oppressive. I raised my daughter in a kind of mutual belonging; I wasn't a possessive mother, but we formed a happy whole. After she left for law school in Paris, I noticed that the living room clock chanted the minutes in a way I didn't like. I'd never heard it before. Weekends were particularly hard for me; I corrected my student's papers in front of the TV. I did have a few friends, but most were in relationships and saw me as a pariah, if not a threat. The few single people in the group reflected an image of myself that I didn't want to face—I knew their answers before they gave them. Gradually, I stopped seeing them, as if to stop seeing myself. So, the weekends without my daughter started to last for a long time. I scheduled our appointments on Friday nights—did you notice? For a long time, I thought the days of the week had an influence over my life. Nothing good could happen before Thursday, whereas Friday was pleasant; there was the promise of a light afternoon. I also liked to associate days with colors. I've often asked the people I like what color they associate with Sunday, Tuesday ... They each give a different response. I've never met a person who thinks the same way I do. You should try it—it tells you a lot about other people. And if we see each other again, I dare to hope that it will be a light blue day and that our days will match.

Here is a sheet of paper that you can fill out to tell me the colors of your life.

Monday...

Tuesday...

Wednesday...

Thursday...

Friday...

Saturday...

Sunday...

That Friday, we held each other's gaze a little longer and you smiled, but it wasn't you being polite—you were showing me that you were happy to see me. I smiled back at you and lay down, trembling with emotion. You made the same gestures as before, at the same speed, in the same order; and yet, there was a different energy in your hands, and it felt like you were touching my skin directly. You actually grazed the skin of my neck, and each of our breathing quickened for an instant.

In the year during which we'd only exchanged a few words, your hands spoke to my body, and it had responded; I'll remember that we all speak the same language, but we're afraid to listen to each other. "Who hears the tree that falls in the forest?" I don't think anyone hears it, but everyone feels it fall. Few people care about trees that fall far away from them, and we refuse to accept the fact that our hearts hear everything. That our humanity is the sum of decimated forests, of trees falling inside us, springs gurgling, birds, cries of pain, and bees buzzing. Isn't that a very Japanese way of thinking? In reading your country's authors, my mind is opening up to another way of seeing life. During my lesson of the day, I learned what a noppera-bô (のっぺら坊) is—a "ghost without a face." Your legendary creatures are terrifying; they look like the moment when day turns into night, like what could be real, what frightens us as children: those shapes in a dark bedroom that often become monsters. The human appearance of the noppera-bô makes the danger omnipresent, and we can suspect it in everyone. From you, I feel nothing but protection; but for some time now, I've been examining people to see if they aren't wearing human masks, because the noppera-bô can make its facial features disappear when it wants and replace them with featureless skin that completely covers what makes us human. From this large expanse of flesh emerges the fear in the eyes of others, and the Japanese ghosts love this. That is what sets us apart because, all too often, I get the feeling that I am one of those ghosts, that my features have drowned in a nothingness that makes me more invisible than frightening. People don't see me, don't recognize me, don't stare at the features on my face, like the way we can never remember the exact color of asphalt. I am a ghost that doesn't frighten, haunted by the memories that it has silenced. Like many of us, my adolescence was a time of vague sorrows. I was floating in sadness when I met the man who got me pregnant; in order to become a woman, something inside me had to cry out. My father didn't know how to love. He was already stooped at thirty, having given up. He even stopped shouting as he got older. It's likely I wanted to awaken his anger the way we want to arouse love. I didn't have the words or the understanding of the world I needed, but I sensed that he was broken. I never knew why. Alcohol kept him company far too often, and my questions, when heard, were mocked. Had I been a boy, it probably would have been different. Daddy only brightened up once a year for the big July 14th carnival. We'd drive towards Lille in the car that had been washed for the occasion. He excelled with a rifle and I can remember the sweet smell of candied apples and the explosions from the fireworks as the only happy sky from my childhood. One sky per year. From the way my father looked bereft at the mere mention of his own childhood, and cut his mother off when she would tell me what he was like as a child, I understood that something was off. And I wanted to protect my father as much as I hated him, because his silence had become my own as he reenacted some of my grandfather's gestures beneath my childhood sheets.

It's ridiculous—I was going to apologize because I've let several days go by without writing to you; as if we were connected by these pieces of paper and you can sense when I'm no longer speaking to you. This invisible thread probably exists between us anyway—what will remain?

I realize that this letter reveals suffering and secrets. I don't want you to think that you are a life preserver; despite the whirlpools of childhood that sometimes sucked me under, I am afloat. But your hands and the feelings they provoked, first in my heart and then throughout my entire soul, forced me to dive beneath the waves and resurface with the beauty and the horror.

I spent the afternoon at my daughter's. Now that she has money, it seems like she's putting distance between us. I can sense it in things that are almost imperceptible: a chin movement, a wave of her hand, the way she looks at me when I wrap up the remains of a meal in aluminum foil. It's as if we were no longer part of the same world, as if she were walking in one of those bubbles that enchant children at carnivals, only hers is magic—she never stumbles in it, and I am the one that seems to belong to a dark and shameful universe. She saw me wring my hands. I felt so awful, so far away. Her husband came home in the evening, and they invited me to stay for dinner. She murmured something in his ear and they laughed; I sensed they were making fun of me. It was probably my shoes or a word I mispronounced. I got up, said I was tired and that I'd be happy to come back another time. My anger was palpable.

"Mom, you should meditate."

In this world of rich people, it seems there is now a mandate for happiness, or a need to show a face that's endlessly smooth. Let's all be plastic dolls!

"I do, before and after my Japanese lessons."

She laughed and then realized it wasn't a joke.

"You're taking Japanese lessons?"

They looked at each other and once again laughed at me in silence.

"And you meditate?"

"Yes, before each lesson."

"You do know that meditation is Indian, don't you?"

"Descartes' metaphysical meditations didn't arrive by way of Bombay, as far as I know."

"We're talking about the thing where you go inside yourself, go quiet, and let go."

"Yes, I know what we're talking about."

"Can you talk to us in Japanese, Alice?"

I insisted on my fatigue and burgeoning migraine and left.

On my way home, I passed the Pont des Arts where lovers come to attach padlocks bearing their initials. Personnel from the mayor's office were clipping them off with wire cutters because the bridge is too heavy and could collapse. I saw the padlocks fall, one after the other, like soldiers sacrificed on the battlefield. Do you think that had any effect on all of those couples? That they argued that day and separated violently? Do you think the mechanics of the unexpected overwhelm our feelings in an irrepressible way? Even when the facts don't clash, when they have nothing to do with each other? The famous flap of a butterfly's wings. Surely, you know the theory well. It comes from a lecture given by Edward Lorenz, in which he asked the question, "Does the flap of a butterfly's wings in Brazil set off a tornado in Texas?" He might have asked if the flap of that same butterfly's wings could prevent a tornado, but drama is more interesting—it's part of humanity. The domino effect ...

Ever since I met you, I've been telling myself that it can lead to bliss. Without my daughter making me move to Paris, without the rain, without the need for me to seek shelter, without that woman who didn't come for her massage, without my fear of saying no, without so many things, I wouldn't have met you. For the Japanese, the butterfly is the symbol for woman, and two butterflies that of marital bliss. That is now how I imagine us at the end of our lives—like those pretty, colorful beings; because we left our cocoons a long time ago, free and happy, drawn to one another for the time of wonder that we have left.

There was the session where we laughed.

My appointment was at the very end of the day. You opened the door of the tea room, which looked like it was closed. Kyoko wasn't there and you had invited me to come directly inside your little house. You went out to give me time to slip on my shiatsu outfit; but when you came back a few minutes later, I wasn't yet ready and you saw me contorting my body. I was trying to reach the zipper on my dress, in vain.

"I help?" you asked, laughing.

"I can't do it," I replied, and then I burst out laughing.

We were like two little kids. And then, suddenly, the laughter stopped.

You came closer and I smelled your particular scent of cedar and paper. I lifted my hair. One of your hands held onto my shoulder while the other gently slid the zipper down.

And we stayed immobile for a while. Then, you went out and I finished undressing in a floating state.

I took off my bra and my nipples were hard. The pajama I slipped on felt as though it were caressing me. You opened the door and I held my breath.

When you put your warm hands on me, I sunk into a state very close to sleep, but that kept me awake for days afterward. Your hands on my body were no longer those of a simple masseur. Our breathing couldn't lie. I dreamt of you all night, half awake, my hands between my thighs. It was a full moon and I was twenty again.

I didn't know how to reach you, otherwise I would have. Spring suddenly arrived and the air was hot. I promised myself I'd go to see you as soon as the tea room opened and kiss you. I was concocting adolescent plans, scenarios in which you dipped my body backward like a movie actress; you kissed me in a hundred different ways before I fell asleep, a smile on my lips.

The telephone rang just as dawn broke. My son-in-law informed me that my granddaughter had been born.

On the morning when I thought I'd join you, put on my young woman's clothes, I woke up a grandmother. The reality of it forced me to put on one skin too many when I was just about to shed one. I felt stuck in my life. I'm ashamed to say it, but I felt no joy. I hate myself for that. I wanted to like myself, after all, so I'd made efforts. Having a granddaughter was an event—surely, the emotion would come naturally. I'd put on black mascara to bring out my eyes and blush on my cheeks. It was only eight o'clock in the morning.

I walked all the way to the hospital. It was fairly far, but springtime was caressing the air with its perfume, and I was discovering Paris in that weather. Hospital visits were limited, and they asked me who I was. When

I said "the grandmother," no one questioned this status and it nearly made me cry. In the elevator, I realized that my daughter was becoming a mother in her own right, and the emotion came. For her.

However, when I walked into the room, Marine looked at me distantly, as if the reserve of love intended for me had diminished and I was now bothersome. I should have immediately transferred what Marine was taking away from me to this little being, whose fragile fingers were holding onto one of mine. I looked at her with her tiny knit cap and her beautifully shaped nose, but felt nothing. I was only thinking that I'd come and kiss you afterward, that I would dare to run to you. The other grandparents arrived. They were more elegant, had the right words, a teddy bear as soft as cashmere, and a luxury brand gift wrapped with a silk bow. I hadn't bought anything before the baby was born—in my family, we said it brought bad luck. But I was carrying Marine's birth bracelet in my pocket. I'd kept it all these years and now brought it in a little leather pouch, like an old coin purse containing a priceless object. I took out my treasure, overwhelmed by what the coming emotion would soon bring me, like a boomerang. When I took the little girl in my arms, I went to put her mother's bracelet on her wrist.

"What are you doing?"

"This was yours."

"It's so dirty, and old. Honey, take the baby, would you?"

The other grandmother grabbed her before her son could react. Marine's birth bracelet was put with the luxury gifts, isolated so as not to spread germs. I was so shocked that transmission wasn't a thing of wonder for my daughter. Had I failed to teach her about what matters? I was once again a spectator, a secondary character, an extra even, since I wasn't allowed to have any lines. I am at an age where you know very well that you only shine if others fade out intermittently in your favor. And for that to happen, they have to love you.

"She's a real Lavilaine," exclaimed the young grandfather, and I realized they all shared the same last name, except for me. I didn't dare take back Marine's little bracelet, but I knew it would be lost, forgotten or thrown away. The power of symbols only has value for those who have lived or are born nostalgic for a forgotten life. That was not the case for any of them. They were in the vulgarity of the present and wondered who the little girl was going to look like while I was imagining her first day of school and her first love. My daughter now seemed to know the price of things, but had forgotten the value of the essential. I put my coat on slowly so that she'd stop me. She didn't. Everyone was looking at the baby.

"What are you going to name her?"

"We haven't decided yet."

"I'll let you get some rest."

There was no protest. I smiled at the baby as if she could sense it, kissed my daughter on the forehead, kissed the cheeks of her husband and his parents, and left.

The hallway was still that of a hospital, and when you've come for a being without a name, seen someone you don't recognize, it makes you very sad. I waited a while for the elevator. Benoît Lavilaine joined me and I jumped.

I was lost in my thoughts and didn't see him coming.

"Ages us, doesn't it ... Well, not you of course, you had Marine young, so ..."

"It's the same for me. It's ... very emotional."

"I don't know if it's Paris, but you've started to sparkle these last few months, you're very beautiful, Alice."

"Thank you."

"You shouldn't stay alone. A man could make you

happy. Even discreetly. I mean, without you having to get remarried and all of that nonsense."

He seemed embarrassed to talk to me about that, and it made me even more uncomfortable. We had only ever exchanged banalities and politeness. The elevator arrived. We were on the ninth floor. At the seventh, Benoît Lavilaine pushed me up against the wall and tried to kiss me. His breath smelled of coffee, and he smelled of vetiver oil. I turned my head and he lifted my skirt.

"No one will find out. Let me."

I slapped him with a strength I never knew I had. It was the first time I'd dared to reject a man. The other times, I'd been so afraid and felt I didn't have the right. The feelings I have for you helped me defend myself. I walked out of the elevator.

"Please, don't say anything. Don't say anything to Catherine. I don't know what came over me. You're not even my type."

He had just definitively excluded me from the family. My daughter no longer understood me, and I didn't feel anything for my granddaughter. Of course, afterward, I couldn't come to see you to kiss you, like in my nighttime fantasies. I felt different and isolated, so I went back home and knocked myself out with a sleeping pill.

When I woke up, I wrote you a first letter and threw it away, like a coward. I sat curled up in a ball in front of my breakfast for hours, trying to find the right words. I'd always corrected papers in my kitchen, as if it were my real place, that of a woman, and I was overstepping my rights by having a job. My mother took odd cleaning jobs left and right, but we didn't say that she worked. She was a housewife like her mother before her. When I was trying to write my novel, I'd curl up in the old chair near the teapot without ever thinking of using the little desk in the living room. My father wasn't thrilled for me to get my diploma, for me to go to university, for me to be an "intellectual," as his friends put it; to him, that was the worst thing for a woman. The more educated I became, the uglier I would be to men. Looking back, I don't think he was entirely wrong; the more power and scope a woman gains, the less desirable she becomes. It's terrible, but that's how it is. I should have thought of being beautiful and hydrating my skin instead of nourishing my mind. I had enticed Benoît Lavilaine because he saw me as some redneck from the countryside; most men need to feel superior in order to feel desire. We do say "possess a woman," don't we?

Since we met, I've been wondering at what point I stopped thinking about my body and pleasing it. How was I able to live inside an envelope that I denied for so many years? Men's eyes, their gestures or their cruel words probably drove me to forget its existence. There was that very tall, skinny boy with green eyes who could switch from the greatest consternation to the greatest violence and had no empathy. He was practically albino with thick lips. He was handsome at first glance, and monstrous when you lingered on his full appearance. He always wore a leather jacket—even on summer days; he thought it made him look good, but it actually only accentuated the deformity of his immense legs.

Nevertheless, I like him. He liked himself as much as others liked him—that's the aura that radiates from self-confident people. We'd been together for several days when he told me, "I don't understand your body." It took me a moment to realize that he thought I was too fat. I left in tears, but he caught up with me and apologized, saying he'd stay and wait for me to lose weight and feel beautiful. Before that, I'd felt neither fat nor ugly. I starved myself, and he congratulated me for every pound I lost. My body shrunk, but my anger grew. Later on, when I realized he was suppressing homosexual urges, I was already damaged. I could slim down, but I couldn't transform into a man. He hit me several times—it never lasted very long—and then he'd apologize. He made love to me in the middle of the night, from behind—he was half-asleep, still foggy from his dreams. I could have been anyone. I stayed for too long, but finally found the strength to leave. For my daughter. So that she would know there was something better.

And for me, better was solitude.

I'm trying to look for happy moments, I don't want you to see me as a ball of sorrow. That stolen night with my friend, Michèle. I was already living at the home and had told them that I was going to try to see my parents. My mother had confirmed it. I think she told herself that now that I was pregnant, nothing worse could happen to me, so, she set me free and helped me in my escapes. Michèle didn't have her license, but her grandmother let her borrow her Peugeot. We drove all the way to the beach and ordered waffles for dinner. I remember a pure, childlike joy. I was going to be a mother, but I wasn't yet an adult. The wind on my face, the freedom, the idea that anything was possible despite the doll that was growing inside my belly. It was also Michèle who went with me to the hospital when I had my first contractions. At eight months pregnant, we were singing *The Final Countdown* at the top of our lungs—that was the hit of the moment. We had no idea what it meant. I now know that final countdown was the one separating my life as a child and the current one. When Marine was born, a lot of questions were answered, and many more arose.

I'd like to tell you about memories I don't yet have. I get the distinct impression that we don't live in chrono-logical order—that time is made of loops. We suddenly recollect certain things that seemed forgotten to us, though we've only just experienced them. And these memories directly affect our present. If that could be true, maybe in some tomorrow yesterday, I'd lie down once again in that little room, you'd smile at me, put your hands on me, and there would only be the present. In the same way that eclipses exist, why wouldn't time go backward? At the University of Princeton, as a birth-day present, a researcher named Kurt Gödel offered Einstein the possible resolution of one of the formulas for time that drew a straight line on which one could likely travel into the past. Anecdotally, the same paranoid mathematician wouldn't eat anything that wasn't prepared by his wife, lest he be poisoned. She was hospitalized for six months, and he died of starvation. Einstein might have taken the time to feed him …

Another connection with you; all of my recurring memories, my desires and my anecdotes are flying over the ocean towards your country of dragons and red lanterns. In 1922, Einstein travelled to Japan and stayed in the Imperial Hotel in Tokyo where a courier brought him a letter … No one knows if the latter refused a tip, as is the custom in your country, or if Albert Einstein had no change; but so as not to let him leave empty-handed, the scientist gave him two notes in German. They weren't mathematical equations, but rather wise words. On one of the papers he'd written: "A quiet and modest life brings more happiness than a pursuit of success bound with constant unrest." On the second was the famous adage taken from Lenin: "Where there's a will, there's a way." I'm holding onto everything that binds my emotions together to believe in a way that will lead us to one another,

I let my letter sit for two days and then reread it—
not without shame. I know I have no other choice but
to continue; but once it's written, will I dare to send it
to you? It's not yet six o'clock in the morning and you're
already in my thoughts or, should I say, you're still in
them because you spent the night in my dreams. Even
though I'm not working anymore, I like to get up early.
When the sky is that black that's not yet blue, when the
night refuses to get up, like a teenager glued to his bed;
I turn on the lights in my apartment and look out the
window. In winter, silhouettes hurry along but evolve
more slowly than they do when, carried by the warmth
of summer dawns, they are airy and cheerful. When
the cold is piercing, I see some of them turn up their

collars and trudge to work. I switch my lights on and off like a lighthouse in the middle of my dark building. My tiny bedside lamp sends a coded message, bolstering their courage. Sometimes I think I see a step lighten at the sight of my signals, like a smile from a body resisting the bite of the icy wind. There are also those that I recognize and that don't touch the ground, despite the exhaustion of staying up all night—the people that have just fallen in love. They are the ones who send light back to me. Would you do that with me one morning? We'll watch the silhouettes. We can laugh, study them, and imagine their secrets so we can confess our own. I'd like to transfer the intimacy of your massages to the center of my life. This garment of flesh and bone is no longer a burden and is becoming a means of telling you about my suffering, my past, my desires. The sensuality that once emanated from me is unraveling, releasing itself beneath your fingers. Some things require no words. What I feel is a language that floats, that we understand without having to look at each other, because, in that room, there is an atmosphere originating from us and surpassing us all at once. With this letter, I am trying to give it names, to articulate sentences, but we probably already know everything instinctively. Why bother writing it? To memorialize this feeling, and so you can dive into it by rereading this letter. Maybe also to build a sort of mausoleum in which to protect my emotions, like so many precious objects? I hope I don't seem strange to you now that you are discovering me beyond what your intuition has told you.

Are there people who feel good? Who endure life as if they were in their rightful place? You struck me as someone who is grounded and capable of healing sorrows with your hands; but can we heal sorrows if they've never passed though us, shaken us, knocked us down? I see the melancholy deep in your eyes, but it seems like you live with it peacefully. How did you manage that? Am I wrong? Do you sometimes weep behind your orange, flowered curtains? Yes, I saw your windows. I know where you live. Please don't think I am crazy. Just a woman whose heart beats in unison with yours. I didn't intend to follow you. One evening, on the way back from dinner at my daughter's place, I saw you on the subway. I wanted to wave to you, but you looked sad and lost in your thoughts, so I resisted. When you got off, I did the same without thinking; like you instinctively cover someone who's cold, I wanted to protect you in my own way.

But just a few meters past the subway exit, you went

into your building. I didn't get the chance to talk to you. Maybe we could have gained days of happiness, or I would have stopped imagining things that didn't exist. I think I didn't want to know. I've always preferred the comfort of fantasy to the risks of life.

You typed your door code quickly—it caught me off guard. I was just behind you, ready to smile at you, but you didn't turn back around. I found myself standing there stupidly, alone on your street. A clear night had just fallen.

I looked up.

The light on the third floor came on and you opened the window. I hid with my back to the street lamp—but I don't think you looked down. You lit a cigarette, and that surprised me. I'd never smelled the odor on your hands or on your breath. I thought you must only smoke occasionally and that I had been right—some sorrow must have overtaken you. I watched your shadow pass. Beneath your windows, my heart beat like a teenager's. The light went out. I thought that you'd maybe seen me and that if I closed my eyes like in the movies, the door would open and you would walk over to me to give me a kiss.

One.

Two.

Three.

I'm ashamed of my naiveté.

Of course, I was alone on that chilly street, but not entirely; you came to live in the house where my dormant hope had been living.

I went home before the subway stopped running, smiling the whole way back.

I woke up with my face on my wooden table, my pen still in my hand. I don't remember falling asleep. Dawn is breaking and I haven't finished this letter. I feel like I have to keep up this momentum; otherwise, I'll never muster the courage to mail it to you. So, I start writing again without eating or drinking, without thinking of anything other than expressing what I've buried since I met you. I trust you. I don't know you; but if you were behind me, I'd let myself fall backward without fear. I know that you'd catch me. I know you will catch me.

A year has gone by. On October 16th, I knew it was my last Japanese lesson. I'd come every evening, even if I was sick—even frightened. The time to speak had arrived. I've entitled myself to so much ever since the day we met: to laugh at movies all night long while eating chips and chocolate cake, to drink late in bars while smiling, to let the wind float up under my skirt. Out of this resurrection a deep feeling has emerged, and now what I want is to live out my peaceful life near you. This morning, I dressed as simply as possible, as if I wanted you to see me naked. Not the kind of nudity that calls for eroticism, but that of the Garden of Eden, pure and undisguised. I wanted you to see me and love me as I am, with the soft wrinkles around my smile, the few blonde eyelashes that frame my eyes, and the childhood that still has a place in part of my silhouette. I came to you.

The last time I'd seen you, you gave me an origami frog made of pink paper ... It fell out of my purse while I was having my Japanese lesson. My teacher told me that "kaeru" meant both "frog" and "to go home." I thought you were opening your arms to me, and I blushed.

Then, he asked me, "What's your Japanese friend's name?" though I'd never even mentioned you. I answered with "Akifumi," and he told me that your name meant "Autumn message." I thought that was so pretty. The leaves were falling in piles, the red and brown ground creating a soft rug on which I could come to you. Everything was in place.

Forgive me, I'm changing the ink color of my letter because I used up an entire pen and all I have left is blue. Should I see that as a sign? It seems like I never saw signs anywhere before knowing you. Now, I'm starting to believe in a kind of mysticism that links souls together and controls colors, the elements, and the growth of flowers.

I hadn't come to the tea room in over a month. I wanted to be ready to sputter in front of you in Japanese. I practiced the words in my head like a refrain.

"Akifumi, watashi was anata to hanasa nakereba narimasen."

In the reflection of the toy store window near my apartment, I looked at myself for a long time, saw myself, and thought that I was pretty. I pulled my hair up in a chignon so that you could admire the neck that your fingers touched so many times.

Men stared at me in the subway. You restored my power to be an object of desire. That pleases and frightens me at the same time.

"Akifumi, I need to speak to you ..."

"Akifumi, watashi wa anata to hanasa nakereba narimasen."

I hoped that the words wouldn't suddenly disappear and that I'd find myself helpless, like Cinderella after the ball.

When I turned onto the street where the tea room is, it was raining. The children from the neighboring school were running in a mad circle. I thought, this is good, it's a cycle—it's just as it was the first time. The sky was surely showing me a sign.

I arrived all wet. I sat down to have a cup of tea and Kyoko gave me a daifukumochi. I thanked her in Japanese and it made her laugh.

I took my time because I knew my life might change forever. I was finally going to tell you things, tell you that I'd learned the words that I needed in order to talk with you.

Kyoko came to get me. My mouth was dry and my hands holding each other. I'd practiced the words several times in my head and in front of the mirror in my bedroom, but they seemed to get jumbled and no longer made any sense. I don't know why I thought I'd see you before, dressed, but I respected the order of things. I took off my clothes and trembled while putting on the navy pajamas. I didn't lie down. I remained seated and hoped that your gaze would immediately soothe me, give me courage. A woman came in. I didn't understand at first. I thought it must be a mishap but, in very good French, she asked me to lie down.

I asked: "Akifumi? Akifumi isn't here?"

"No, I'm his replacement."

"Is he OK? Will he be back soon?"

"Akifumi doesn't work here anymore."

It was indeed a cycle. I heard the rain and, once again, tears ran down my face. They expressed pain and anger, the injustice of fate. "Unmei"—that word suddenly became ugly. And I felt ridiculous for having imagined some connection between us. I muttered some excuse to put my clothes back on. I was ashamed. Each of my movements unmasked me even more.

"I have the same training, don't worry."

"I'm sorry, I have to go."

I left without even completely buttoning my blouse. I was out of breath. Kyoko explained to me that you had gone back to Japan. I asked if you were joining someone and she answered, "No, Akifumi alone, always alone." And instead of comforting me, this plunged me into an infinite sadness. We are alike and alone. The frog meant that you were going back home, and that it was far, very far from me. I wasn't your new home as I had very much hoped.

That was three months ago.

Apparently, the tea room has been sold. The last time I went, Kyoko gave me your address and gave me a hug. Women understand the silences of the heart.

Mine derailed a few days ago when I passed in front of the tea room and all that remained was the iron curtain. I'd put my sorrows away in the drawer of my dreams from which you sometimes reappeared joyfully; at night, we loved each other but, in the morning, it was awful. And now the tea room, whose name was gone from the façade, made me question everything. Did you really exist?

It was a beautiful day. The children from the neighboring school must have been in class because you couldn't hear any noise. The tea room had just been repainted; it was a white, empty space. Everything seemed to tell me that I had maybe imagined it all, that the only joyful reality of my final years had been erased. I went closer and saw my face in the reflection on a part of the store window. My body swayed, and then nothing.

When I woke up at the hospital, I felt happy. My pain had finally produced a symptom, and someone was caring for me.

It's ironic—it's the Japanese who named my illness: a tako-tsubo. It means "octopus trap" because the heart swells on the left side and takes on the same shape. It isn't a heart attack; there is no blood clot. They say that it's brought on by stress—that word we use for everything. I have a more humane vision. I think you can have a broken heart—it doesn't matter what constitutes the grief, lost love, violence, fear—when you get too strong a dose of anguish and pain, the heart becomes deformed and you collapse.

That's what happened to me.

Did you know that the heart scars? I will always have a physical memory that streaks mine; a trace of the pain that knocked me down. If you look closely, perhaps it'll be your first name, or the coordinates of your birthplace.

I wonder how your heart is doing.

I spoke with the doctor for a long time and he suggested that I write you this letter. He told me that at the end, I'd see if it felt necessary to mail it, but that I should put the emotion that you sparked in me down on paper. I can't keep the desire for us locked inside me.

Writing to you is all I have left. Writing this letter and waiting for a response to come so I can visit you in Myazaki. Don't laugh at me, but I've never taken an airplane. My grandfather was in the French airmail service. He died in an airplane crash. I had just been born. My father never looked up at the sky again and cut trees so he could look downward. He didn't believe in God. Anything that could leave solid ground scared him: dreams, music, bottles in the sea, love. All of that was forbidden to me. The only poetry in my life was gardening. Planting flowers and watching them reveal their magical colors before dying without ever being

93

able to run from our garden. Rooted, as if in prison, like I was. I learned that, in Japan, you have a flower for every month. And even a verb that means "to look at flowers." If you let me come see you next month, I could discover the famous April cherry trees. I imagine myself running through a pink tunnel, and I hope that you're waiting for me at the other end. This morning, I read in the paper that the padlocks from the Pont des Arts will be sold at auction, in bunches. Hundreds of padlocks like so many unkept promises. I hope they don't slow down my momentum with their wretched weight.

I was told that in Japan, people who love each other don't declare themselves. That you talk of love all around, love as something that transcends beings, surrounds them, reveals them, or crushes them. You don't say "I love you," but rather, "there is love," like there is sunshine.

I don't know if you'll want to see me again or write to me. My name and address are on the back of this envelope, and my entire life is inside. I am prepared for you to do nothing with it.

Still, I hope that you'll understand what I'm not telling you.

Alice

Amanda Sthers was born in Paris and lives in Los Angeles. She is the bestselling author of fourteen novels; after her American debut with *Holy Lands*, she adapted her best seller *Love Alice* for her English readers. She is also a playwright, screenwriter, and director. In 2011, the French government named her a Chevalier (Knight) in the Ordre des Arts et des Lettres, the highest honor it bestows on artists, for her significant and original contributions to the literary arts.